Can You Solve the Mystery?

Hawkeye Collins & Amy Adams in
The Case of the
Video Game
Smugglers
& 9 Other Mysteries

Created by Bruce Lansky

 Meadowbrook Press
Distributed by Simon & Schuster
New York

Library of Congress Cataloging-In-Publication Data

This title was previously cataloged with the following information: Masters, M.
Hawkeye Collins & Amy Adams in the case of the video game smugglers and other mysteries.
At head of title: Can you solve the mystery?
Summary: Hawkeye Collins and Amy Adams, two twelve-year-old sleuths,
solve ten mysteries using Hawkeye's sketches of important clues. The reader is
invited to use Hawkeye's sketches to solve the mystery.
[1. Mystery and detective stories. 2. Literary recreations.] I. Title. II. Title:
Case of the video game smugglers and other mysteries.
PZ7.M42392Hf   1983   [Fic] 83-902

ISBN: 978-1-4424-6901-3

Editor: Kathe Grooms
Assistant Editor: Louise Delagran, Alicia Ester
Cover Design: Tamara JM Peterson
Design: Stephen Cardot, Terry Dugan
Production: John Ware, Donna Ahrens, Pamela Barnard, Daryl Peterson
Illustrations: Stephen Cardot
Interior Hand Photography: Tamara JM Peterson
Hand Model: Emily Peterson
All stories written by Alexander von Wacker

20 19 18 17 16 15 14   15 14 13 12 11 10 9 8 7 6 5 4 3

Printed in USA

Contents

Amy Adams   Hawkeye Collins

Young Sleuths Detect Fun in Mysteries

By Alice Cory
Staff Writer

Lakewood Hills has two new super sleuths watching over its citizens. They are Christoper "Hawkeye" Collins and Amy Amanda Adams, both 12 years old and sixth-grade students at Lakewood Hills Elementary.

Christopher Collins, the popular, blond, blue-eyed sleuth of 128 Crestview Drive, is better known by his nickname, "Hawkeye." His father, Peter Collins, who is an attorney downtown, explains, "We started calling him Hawkeye many years ago because he notices everything, even tiny details. That's what makes him so good at solving mysteries." His mother, Linda Collins, a real estate agent, agrees: "Yes, but he

Sleuths continues on page 4A

Sleuths continued from 1A

also started to draw at a very early age. His sketches capture everything he sees. He draws clues or the scene of the crime — or anything else that will help solve a mystery."

Amy Adams, a spitfire with red hair and sparkling green eyes, lives right across the street, at 131 Crestview Drive. Known to many as the star of the track team, she is also a star math student. "She's quick of mind, quick of foot and quick of temper," says her teacher, Ted Bronson, chuckling. "And she's never intimidated." Not only do she and Hawkeye share the same birthday, but also the same love of mysteries.

"If something's wrong," says Amy, leaning on her bike, "you just can't look the other way."

"Right," says Hawkeye, pulling his ever-present sketch pad and pencil from his back pocket. "And if we can't solve a case right away, I'll do a drawing of the scene of the crime. When we study my sketch, we can usually figure out what happened."

When the two detectives are not playing video games or soccer (Hawkeye is the captain of the sixth-grade team), they can often be seen biking around town, making sure justice is done. Occa-sionally aided by Hawkeye's frisky golden retriever, Nosey, and Amy's six-year-old sister, Lucy, they've solved every case they've handled to date.

How did the two get started in the detective business?

It all started last year at Lakewood Hills Elementary's Career Days. There the two met Sergeant Treadwell, one of Lakewood Hills' best-known policemen. Of Hawkeye and Amy, Sergeant Treadwell proudly brags, "They're terrific. Right after we met, one of the teachers had a whole pile of tests stolen. I sure couldn't figure out who had done it, but Hawkeye did one of his sketches and he and Amy had the case solved in five minutes! You can't fool those two."

Sergeant Treadwell adds: "I don't know what Lakewood Hills ever did without Hawkeye and Amy. They've found a dognapped dog, located stolen video games, and cracked many other tough cases. Why, whenever I have a problem I can't solve, I know just where to go — straight to those two super sleuths!"

> **" They've found a dognapped dog, located stolen video games, and cracked many other tough cases.''**

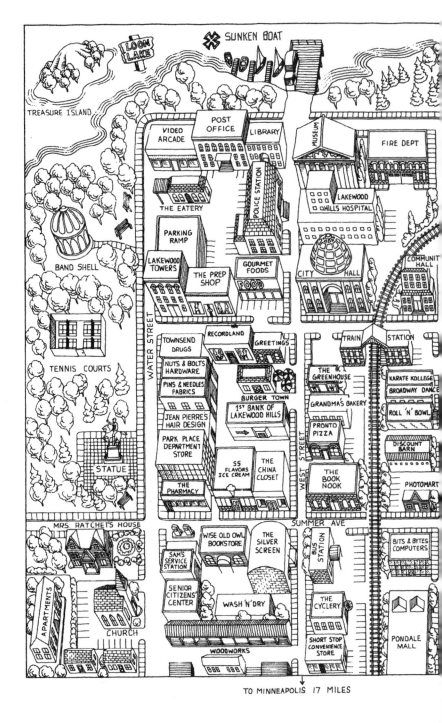

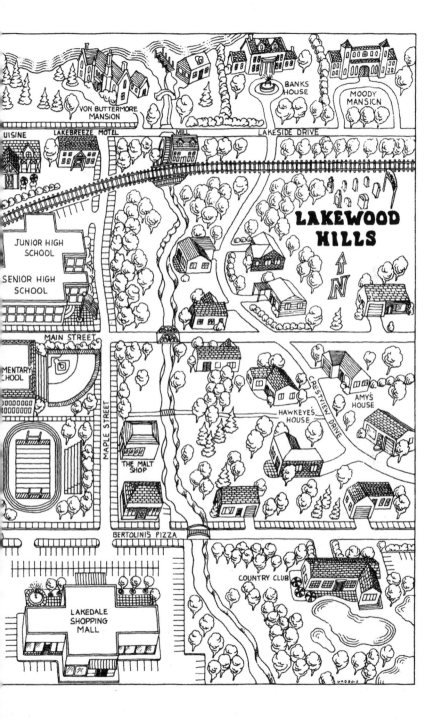

Dear Readers,

You can solve these mysteries along with us! Start by reading very carefully -- Watch out for things like what people <u>say</u> happened, the ways they behave, and details like the time and the weather.

Then look closely at the sketch or other picture clue with the story. If you remember the facts, the picture clue should help you break the case.

If you want to check your answer -- or if a hard case stumps you -- turn to the solutions at the back of the book. They're written in mirror type. Hold them up to a mirror and they'll look right. If you don't have a mirror, turn the page and hold it up to the light. (You can teach yourself to read backwards, too. We can do it pretty well now and it comes in handy some-times in our cases.)

Have fun -- we sure did!

Hawkeye   Amy

The Case of the
Computer Camp Kidnap

Ready for computer camp, Hawkeye Collins carried his suitcase and backpack out of his bedroom. Nosey, his frisky golden retriever, sniffed Hawkeye's things, not quite sure what to make of it all.

"Nosey, get my windbreaker over there on the bed," said Hawkeye as he reached the bedroom door. "Go on, get it."

Nosey hesitated a moment, then ran over and took the red windbreaker in her mouth.

"Good girl."

The two of them made their way down the hall and to the front door. Hawkeye put his bags down and took the windbreaker from the dog's mouth.

"Mom, Dad!" he called. "I'm all set!"

His mother finished speaking with one of her real estate clients on the phone and came out of the living room. His father, who had been preparing for a court case, came out of the study, a stack of papers under his arm.

His mother patted his blonde hair. "We're going to miss you."

"Aw, Mom." Hawkeye shrugged. "I'm only going to be gone a week."

"Hey," said his father, "what's Amy going to do while you're gone? Hold down the detective business?"

Amy was Hawkeye's friend and fellow sleuth from across the street. They made a great team, with his eye for detail and ability to draw so well, and her speed and quick mind.

"No," said Hawkeye. "She and her kid sister Lucy are going with their parents up to their Uncle Rick's cabin."

"Things are sure going to be quiet around the neighborhood," said his mother, smiling.

Hawkeye glanced out the window and saw a brown car turn off Crestview Drive and pull into their driveway. It was his ride to camp.

"Hey, Paul and his dad are here!"

Hawkeye scrambled to get his things, checked his back pocket to make sure he had his sketch pad and pencil, and said good-bye to his parents.

"And you be good," he said to Nosey. Hawkeye looked up at his father and noticed his empty suit coat pocket. "Dad, your glasses."

Mr. Collins felt the coat pocket and grinned. "I would have been in court with no glasses today if it weren't for you. You know, sometimes I find it hard to believe we ever named you Christopher. Your nickname suits you so well."

They helped Hawkeye out to the car with his luggage and said their final goodbyes. Hawkeye couldn't wait to get to computer camp, and it seemed like forever before they were on their way.

Hawkeye and his friend, Paul Shimamoto, sat in the back seat and took turns playing a game on Paul's father's cell phone. As they drove along, Paul's father, a computer engineer, told them about the camp.

"Boys," he said, "one of the best things about this camp is that you each have your own laptop."

"Yeah, and in the afternoon we get to play games on them!" said Paul.

Mr. Shimamoto, who had helped set up the camp, was amused. "That's right. But try to learn something more than games. It's a very good opportunity to learn a lot about programming."

Mr. Shimamoto talked more about computers until they arrived at the camp. They said good-bye excitedly, and went straight to their cabins.

That afternoon, the camp staff gave all the boys and girls a tour and showed them all the computers and equipment.

In the evening, after a hot dog roast on the lake shore, there were some meetings and more introductions, and then everyone went for a swim. The campers went to bed early, excited about classes starting the next morning.

But when roll call was taken in the first class, Paul did not answer when his name was called. One of the instructors sent Hawkeye and Anne, the girl sitting beside him, to go find him.

"Paul must still be asleep," said the instructor.

"We're in the same cabin," said Hawkeye. "I know he's up because I saw him this morning. And he ate breakfast at my table. But we'll find him—wherever he is."

Hawkeye and Anne checked the dining room, but it was deserted. The cook was the only person in the kitchen, and he hadn't seen Paul, either.

"Maybe he's sick and he went back to bed or something," said Hawkeye. "Let's go check the cabin."

"Yeah, he's probably back there snoozing," said Anne.

But the cabin was empty and dead silent.

"I wonder where we should look next," said Anne.

Hawkeye went over to Paul's bed. On top of his sleeping bag was a message written in Paul's handwriting.

Hawkeye read through the note. "Oh, no!" he shouted. "Paul's been kidnapped!"

Anne hurried over and read through the ransom note. "What do they mean about bringing plans?"

Hawkeye thought hard for a moment.

"Paul's father is working on an important new computer—the fastest in the whole world," he said. "The kidnappers must want the plans to that computer."

"Come on, Hawkeye," said Anne, "we've got to go get help."

"Hang on a second."

Hawkeye studied the letter a moment, and then pulled his sketch pad and pencil out of his back pocket. There was something odd there. Squinting at the paper, Hawkeye looked for clues. "Boy, I wish Amy were here—she's good at this sort of thing," he said.

He doodled on his pad for a moment, the seed of an idea taking root. He suddenly stopped doodling, quickly jotted down a series of letters, then snapped his fingers.

"Anne—run to the office and have them call the police," said Hawkeye. "I know where the kidnappers have hidden Paul!"

WHERE WERE PAUL AND THE KIDNAPPERS?

Find the solution on page 79

to paul's father
HAVE your soN.
Must cOme To gEt.
Leave police out.
Ransom is Master
plan Of NEw
com puter.
we mean business
will call.

On top of his sleeping bag was a message.

The Secret of the Tomato Pincher

On a pleasant, early fall evening, Hawkeye and Amy, his friend and fellow sleuth from across the street, were walking home after a soccer game.

Hawkeye kicked the soccer ball up into the freshly cut grass of Amy's yard. The two of them, wearing warm-up suits, jogged after it. Amy's red pigtails bounced as she ran.

"I want to play another game," she said. "But, well, it's Sunday night. Time for homework." She reached the ball and kicked it ahead.

"Ugh. Math." Hawkeye stopped running and pushed back his glasses. He was a whiz at computer programming, history, and art, but he had a hard time with math.

"Mom and Dad say I'd do better at math if I only studied a little more," he said, "so that's what they're making me do. An extra—"

"Snakes alive!" cried Amy, who was into unusual expressions. "The tomato thief is back!"

Lurking in the family garden behind the Adams house was a shadowy figure.

"After him!"

Running at full speed and screaming at the top of her lungs, Amy dashed toward the garden. Hawkeye, a bit confused, hesitated but then tore after her.

"You bum! You creep!" shouted Amy. "Those are my family's tomatoes. We grew 'em from seeds. Leave 'em alone!"

The dark figure broke into a mad run. He disappeared around a tree and past a house, as Amy raced after him.

"Get him, Amy!" shouted Hawkeye. "You're the star of the track team. You can catch him!"

"I'm going to find that sucker. He ripped off our biggest tomatoes."

Hawkeye jogged through her yard, past the garden, and into the next yard. He caught up with Amy near some houses on the next street over. She stood leaning against a fence post, trying to catch her breath.

"He... he was really fast," she gasped. "I... I lost him."

Just then they heard a nearby door slam. They both froze and listened, but all was silent.

Hawkeye pointed to a row of four houses across the street. "It came from one of them."

"It sure did." Amy marched forward. "If nothing else, I'm going to warn everyone in those four houses that there's a tomato thief on the loose. And if the thief lives in one of those four houses, then at least he'll know I'm watching for him. He'd better not come back to *my* garden."

Her fists clenched, Amy stomped off.

"You sure are angry," said Hawkeye.

"You can say that again."

Hawkeye grinned. "You sure are—"

"Spare me your intelligent humor," snapped Amy.

The two friends headed across the street and approached the first house. They both knew the woman who came to the door. Hawkeye got out his sketch pad to take notes while Amy warned her of the neighborhood thief.

"Amy, does he also go after broccoli?" asked the woman.

Amy made a face. "Who'd want to steal that?"

"Well, if he only goes after tomatoes, I'm safe. I'm not growing any this year."

A huge college football player lived in the second house. He was easily twice as big as Hawkeye and Amy combined, and he had a voice like a volcano.

"Guys, the only tomatoes I got are in cans. And I don't think nobody's gonna come breakin' in here for canned tomatoes. What d'ya think, kid?" he said, patting Hawkeye on the head, hard.

"I... I think you have a very good point," said Hawkeye, uncomfortably. Amy grinned at Hawkeye but said nothing.

Hawkeye and Amy went on to the third house. A high school kid who had a reputation as a trouble-maker came to the door.

Her fists clenched, Amy said, "There's a tomato thief in the neighborhood."

"So?" said the high school kid.

"You don't know anything about it, do you?" asked Amy.

Something about the guy made Hawkeye distrust him. He stepped back a couple of feet and eased his sketch pad out of his back pocket. Without taking his eyes off the troublemaker's face, he started to sketch him and the room behind him.

The kid wiped his nose. "Nope," he said sullenly.

"Well, if you have a garden, you'd better keep an eye on it," said Amy.

"We don't."

Amy scratched her head. "Are you sure you don't know anything about a tomato thief? I just chased someone over this way."

"Listen, shrimp, I said no. I haven't been out all evening." He turned and pointed into his house. "As you can see, I've just been sittin' around, watchin' TV and eatin' my supper. Heck, I don't even like tomatoes. I'm allergic to 'em."

The kid slammed the door in their faces. Hawkeye and Amy started to walk back to Amy's house.

"He sure is mean. I hope that's not what high school does to you," said Amy.

"Amy," said Hawkeye, "let's go get that football player."

Amy stood stock still. "Hawkeye, if he did it, then he can *have* the tomatoes. In fact, I'll bring him some more."

"No, Amy, you don't get it," said Hawkeye. "We need his help to nail this creep."

"What are you talking about?" asked Amy.

Hawkeye held up a drawing. "I drew this sketch while that kid was talking. Just look at it and you'll see what I mean."

WHY DID HAWKEYE THINK THE HIGH SCHOOL KID HAD STOLEN THE TOMATOES?

Find the solution on page 81

Without taking his eyes off the troublemaker's face,
Hawkeye started to sketch.

The Mystery of the
Unknown
Rescuer

"Hawkeye and Amy, I'm left totally in the dark, so to speak."

Mrs. von Buttermore touched her bandaged forehead. "I got such a nasty bump that I'm not really sure what happened. At the very least, I'd like to write a thank-you letter to the person who helped me out of the Lakewood Hills Public Library. As you know, all the lights went out during the storm, and I have no idea who rescued me."

Hawkeye and Amy sat with Mrs. von Buttermore, the richest person around, in the drawing room of her mansion. She wore a pale green Japanese kimono she had bought on one of her round-the-world trips. Hawkeye and Amy, both dressed in cotton sweaters, jeans, and running shoes, felt a little out of place.

The two sleuths had been to the hilltop mansion before. The first time they were there, they had helped to solve a diamond theft. Since then, Mrs. von Buttermore had called on them whenever something mysterious happened, and the three had become good friends.

"After you called me this morning," began Hawkeye, a drawing in his hand, "I went down to the library and drew a floor plan of the basement level." He liked the plan he had drawn. He thought that if he didn't become a detective when he grew up, maybe he'd be an architect instead.

"The floor plan should help, but why don't we start at the beginning?" said Amy. "Tell us everything."

"Yes, well, I visited the library the other morning to donate the rest of my great-great-great grandpapa's rare books to their collection. As you know, the Rare Books room is in the basement of the library. I entered the building ahead of my chauffeur and some other people who carried the boxes of books."

Hawkeye checked the floor plan. "You went in through the front entrance?"

"Oh, yes."

"Did you talk to anyone?" asked Amy.

"Why, yes, I did, as a matter of fact. I talked to lots of people. When I first entered the building, I greeted the guard. Then I said hello to the librarians. Then I gave a big hug to each of the adorable children who were visiting the library for their very first time. There must have been about twenty of them."

"And then?" asked Hawkeye.

"Then I started going downstairs."

"Which stairs?" Amy scratched her head. "Front or back?"

"Let me see..." Mrs. von Buttermore thought for a moment. "Front. And by that time, my rare books had already been delivered to the Rare Books room. On the way down, I stopped on the landing and chit-chatted with the janitor."

Mrs. von Buttermore squinted slightly, trying to remember what had happened. "Then I said hello to another librarian who came by. At the bottom of the stairs, I spoke with the woman at the information desk—she knows everything and has the nicest seeing-eye dog. I gave her dog a big hug."

Hawkeye wasn't sure if he could keep all this straight. He drew a dotted line tracing Mrs. von

Buttermore's path on his plan of the library. His eyes still on the plan, he said, "Okay, go on."

"As you know, a tremendous storm blew up just after I got to the basement." Mrs. von Buttermore touched the bandage on her forehead. "Why, I was just walking down the hall to the Rare Books room when it started thundering to beat the egg."

"You mean," said Hawkeye, "to beat the band. Thundering to beat the band. Isn't that what you mean?"

"Oh, yes, of course." Mrs. von Buttermore tapped her forehead. "This little bump has gotten me a bit scrambled."

Amy looked at her bump. "Yeah, it sure looks mean."

"Anyway," said Mrs. von Buttermore, pulling at her diamond earring, "I could hear the rain and thunder even down there in the basement. Oh, it was so terrible. Such a bad storm! And then, a gigantic bolt of lightning struck the library itself. Why, Hawkeye and Amy, the whole building nearly jumped right out of the ground!"

"Is that when the lights went out?"

"Yes. Every one of them. Even the emergency lights. It was totally black. Not a bit of light, you know, because I was downstairs and there wasn't a single window."

Mrs. von Buttermore's eyes grew wide with excitement. "At first I stood still, because I couldn't see a thing. But then I began to walk. And I didn't take more than two steps before I tripped over something—a box or something—a box, I think. Why, I fell and hit my head!"

Hawkeye knew the rest of the story. "That's when someone came to you, helped you up, and led you back upstairs and to the main entrance. Right?"

"Yes. In the dark. Can you imagine?"

"But you didn't even get a look at the person?" asked Amy.

"No, unfortunately not. I bumped my head pretty hard and I was rather mixed-up about everything. I couldn't see and I couldn't think clearly, either. And all the little kids were crying—it was quite an uproar.

"All I remember is the pain," she continued. "Whoever helped me just disappeared once I got to the doorway. Then someone else called an ambulance and I was whisked away."

"How about the library? Have you asked if anyone there knows who helped you?" asked Hawkeye.

"Yes, I have. I've called the library several times, but no one has any idea who helped me. There was so much confusion."

Mrs. von Buttermore held up her hands helplessly. "I just want to write that person a thank-you letter and invite him or her to a little banquet or something. But maybe it was someone who doesn't work at the library. Maybe I'll never discover who helped me."

Hawkeye and Amy both turned to the floor plan and ran their eyes along Mrs. von Buttermore's route. They thought of everything she had said, and mentally explored the library. Several minutes later, Hawkeye snapped his fingers and looked up, a big smile on his face.

"It's no dark secret anymore, Mrs. von Buttermore," he said. "I'm pretty sure I know who it is that you can thank for helping you."

WHO HELPED MRS. VON BUTTERMORE WHEN THE LIGHTS WENT OUT?

Find the solution on page 83

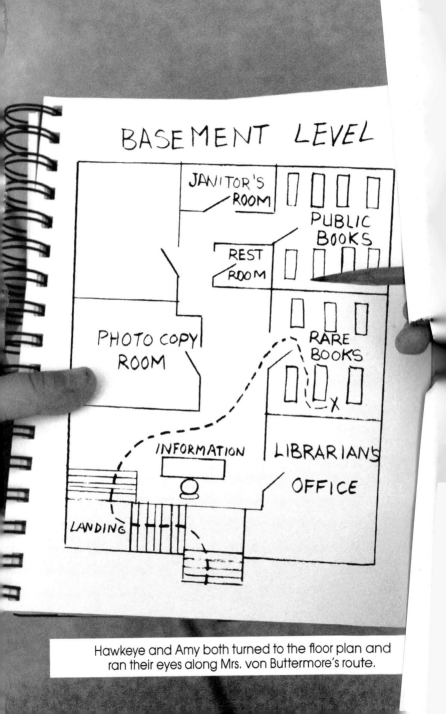

BASEMENT LEVEL

JANITOR'S ROOM

PUBLIC BOOKS

REST ROOM

PHOTO COPY ROOM

RARE BOOKS

X

INFORMATION

LIBRARIAN'S OFFICE

LANDING

Hawkeye and Amy both turned to the floor plan and ran their eyes along Mrs. von Buttermore's route.

The Case of the
Video Game Smugglers

The tires screeched against the pavement as Sergeant Treadwell's police car roared around the corner. In the back seat, Hawkeye and Amy tried to brace themselves as the squad car swerved from side to side.

They came to a straightaway and Sergeant Treadwell pressed on the gas pedal and zoomed even faster toward the airport. The reason: the Digital Thieves had struck again. This time, all copies of The Electric Noodle had been stolen.

"I gave my idea for a meatball and spaghetti video game to the computer club," moaned Hawkeye. "We just finished programming the master yesterday, and today it gets ripped off!"

"It sure is rotten to steal. And particularly from kids," said Sergeant Treadwell. "We're just lucky that one of the thieves' ex-partners thinks so, too. Otherwise, we wouldn't have gotten the tip that they'll be on the four o'clock flight leaving town."

"If they're the two creeps who were hanging around the school, I might be able to recognize them." Amy shook her head. "It was awful to come back to the computer lab and find the flash drive missing and that goony message on the screen. 'Deny access,' indeed!"

Sergeant Treadwell pulled into a side entrance of the airport. He drove up to the terminal and brought the squad car to a quick halt in front of a service door.

"I just hope you'll be able to spot them, Amy," he said, glancing in the rear view mirror. "Three other people have had their video game ideas stolen. The last robbery was five months ago. I chased the crooks out to the airport, but they had disguises on, and they got away."

"Where did you lose them?" asked Hawkeye.

"Somewhere around the metal detector. But we did get a picture of two possible suspects."

Sergeant Treadwell reached into his pocket and pulled out a picture. "Here, my undercover agent took this. These two guys didn't want their camera bags x-rayed. We thought maybe they had flash drives somewhere in the bags, and they were afraid the x-rays would mess them up."

Amy studied the picture. "Did they ask to have visual checks?"

Sergeant Treadwell nodded. "Yep. But no sign of the stolen video game was found. That's why we didn't arrest them."

The sergeant climbed out of the car and headed for the door of the two-story building. Hawkeye and Amy quickly followed.

"I'm going to put on my own disguise," said Sergeant Treadwell, smiling, as he started to walk into a restroom.

Hawkeye said, "We'll go on up and wait for you by the metal detector."

"All right. But don't do anything. Just let me know if you see them."

"Right," said Amy.

Hawkeye and Amy climbed up the back staircase and entered a large corridor. Within a few minutes, they had staked out the airport's metal detector. Sketch pad in hand, Hawkeye sat on a bench. Amy stood over by a candy machine, pretending that she couldn't decide what to buy.

Moments later, Sergeant Treadwell came down the corridor wearing a grey wig, a glued-on, bushy moustache, wire-rimmed glasses, and a checkered vest that didn't quite make it around his pudgy stomach.

"Boy, you look ridiculous," said Hawkeye, smiling as the sergeant approached him.

"Shh!" Sergeant Treadwell said, touching his finger to his fake moustache. "You don't know me, remember?"

Hawkeye laughed. "That's right. I wouldn't want to be seen with someone as silly-looking as you."

"Hey, this is a good disguise. I don't want the thieves to recognize me."

"Well, I don't think they will." Hawkeye shook his head in frustration and anger. "Boy, I sure hope we can get our video game back."

"I do, too, Hawkeye." Sergeant Treadwell looked up and down the hall. "Okay, now, you've got the photograph, right?"

"Right here," said Hawkeye. "I'm going to sketch everyone who has a camera bag and asks for a visual check. Then I'll compare my drawings with your photographs of suspects."

"Good. You just let me know if you spot them." Sergeant Treadwell shuffled away and took up his post down the hall.

Putting the photo to one side, Hawkeye propped up his sketch pad as if he were doing homework. Even if the thieves were wearing disguises, he figured, there had to be something he could recognize.

People bustled up to the scanner and put their bags and packages on the conveyor belt to be checked. All at once, three men who had arrived separately lined up to have their camera bags checked by the guards.

Hawkeye tensed. Biting his bottom lip, he did three separate sketches of the men. Then another man joined the line. A few seconds later, Amy left the candy machine and drifted by Hawkeye.

"Check out the guy in the sunglasses and the chubby guy with the shoulder bag," she said quickly, without stopping.

"Right," murmured Hawkeye, not raising his head. "What about the guy who's being checked right now? Can you get a close look at him—maybe even look in his bag?"

"Will do."

Amy walked over to the line of people. Suddenly, she dropped a handful of change and it all went rolling up to the table where the bags were being checked.

"My money, my money!" she hollered, waving her hands in the air. "I washed dishes for that money! I want it back!"

She dove into the crowd of people and everyone stopped still. Hawkeye tried not to laugh out loud as the people watched Amy scramble around on her knees. She stuck her head up once, glanced into the open camera case on the table, and then ducked down again in search of her money.

Amy wandered by a few minutes later. "That guy sure didn't look familiar. And the only thing I saw in his camera case was a camera."

"Rats."

A few minutes later, Hawkeye had done two more sketches of men who had had their camera bags searched. There was no one else at the metal detector.

All in all, he had six drawings. He picked up the photo and compared it with his sketches.

"If the thieves are here, I should be able to figure out who they are." Hawkeye tapped his pencil on his head. "And I've got to try to figure out where they have the flash drive hidden."

His eyes carefully went back and forth between his drawings of the six men and the photo. Gradually, he began to notice some similar things.

"That nose is familiar. And so are those eyes. That's it!" he gasped. "There's one of them."

"Hawkeye," said Sergeant Treadwell, approaching him, "I haven't spotted either of the suspects. And so far there's no sign of the stolen video game!"

Angrily, the sergeant ripped off the fake moustache glued to his upper lip. "Ahhh!" he cried in pain.

"Wait a minute, Sarge," said Hawkeye. "Look at this. Compare your photograph and my sketches."

Sergeant Treadwell examined them. "Yeah, well... uh-huh... I see." He scratched his head. "Hawkeye, what are you getting at? You're the one with the great eyes. Tell me."

"Oh, come on, Sarge, look!" Hawkeye pointed to two people in the drawings. Then, suddenly, he slapped his forehead. "Oh, wow! Look, here's where the flash drive with the video game is hidden!"

WHO WERE THE VIDEO GAME SMUGGLERS AND WHERE HAD THEY HIDDEN THE DRIVE?

Find the solution on page 85

Suspect X

Suspect Y

"I'll compare my drawings to your photographs of the suspects," said Hawkeye.

The Mystery at Mill Creek Bridge

Pedaling as fast as they could, Hawkeye and Amy raced across the grassy field and down to Mill Creek Lane on the way to school. They were late for soccer practice and this was a good shortcut.

"I'm gonna beat you, Hawkeye!" shouted Amy, her red hair blowing in the wind.

Hawkeye smiled as he leaned over the handlebars. "Never!"

They left a trail of dust on the deserted dirt road. As they approached the old, wooden Mill Creek Bridge, Amy pulled into the lead. Then, suddenly, they heard a cry for help.

"What was that?" said Hawkeye, jamming on the brakes.

Amy slid to a stop ahead of him and looked from side to side. "I heard it, too. Sounded like someone in trouble."

"Oh, help!" cried a small voice.

"Down there," said Hawkeye. "It came from the river."

"Help!" came the boy's voice again. "I'm hurt. Over here, near the bridge."

Hawkeye and Amy hurried to the bridge and saw Jamie Campbell below. The young boy, a neighborhood kid a few grades below them, lay on the shore of the river, hugging one knee, his face twisted in pain. His dirt bike lay on the riverbank.

"Hawkeye, Amy!" called the boy with relief. "I was riding across the bridge and I hit some sand or something. I went flying right off the edge. Oh, my knee!"

"I'll go get help," said Hawkeye.

"No dice," said Amy, hopping back on her bike. "I was beating you, remember? You stay here with Jamie and I'll go get his mom."

Hawkeye grinned. "Oh, all right."

As Amy took off, Hawkeye scrambled down the riverbank to Jamie.

"Don't move your knee," said Hawkeye. "Just lie still. Amy went for help. She'll be right back with your mother."

"I hope Mom won't be mad," said Jamie, sounding worried.

"Why should she be?"

"Because I was supposed to go to choir practice."

Hawkeye pointed to Jamie's knee. "An accident is an accident."

"Yeah, but…" Jamie shrugged. "Mom really likes me to go to practice."

Just then they heard another group of kids racing toward the bridge on their way to school.

Hawkeye got up. "I'd better warn those kids to be careful when they go across the bridge. We don't want another accident."

He clambered up the bank to the road and shouted, "Hey, guys, watch out!" Heeding Hawkeye's warning, a group of five kids coasted cautiously over the bridge.

"I don't know what Jamie hit," said one of the kids, "but I sure don't see anything."

Hawkeye looked around. "I don't, either. Something's strange here."

After the kids were gone, Hawkeye checked the bridge for a rock or a branch or a patch of sand. He found nothing. Determined to solve the mystery, he took out his sketch pad and pencil. From the bridge, he drew what he saw below.

"Hawkeye," called the boy from the shore of the creek, "what are you doing?"

"Just figuring something out," answered Hawkeye, as he studied the scene of the accident.

"Oh..."

A moment later, Hawkeye completed his drawing. He ran down the bank and showed it to Jamie.

"Jamie, why don't you tell me what's going on here?" Hawkeye said.

WHAT REALLY HAPPENED AT THE MILL CREEK BRIDGE?

Find the solution on page 89

"I don't know what Jamie hit," said one of the kids,
"but I sure don't see anything."

The Secret of the
Author's
Autograph

One rainy afternoon, Hawkeye and Amy stopped
by the Wise Owl Used Bookstore. Dimly lit, the
store was filled with ladders on wheels and tall
shelves packed with dusty books. It was famous
for its collection of used comic books and rare
children's books.

Glancing up from a stack of comics, Hawkeye
spotted a row of books by his favorite author.

"Mark Twain!" he exclaimed. Hawkeye rolled
the ladder over and climbed up. "Cool. Hey, Amy,
look at all these books by Mark Twain."

But Amy, sitting on the floor with her legs crossed, couldn't move. She sat glued to a comic book about a trio of superwomen.

"Amy," he repeated, "come over here. Wow! Look at this neat old copy of *Tom Sawyer*! This is what I want."

Hawkeye gently pulled his favorite book from the tall shelf. He climbed down the ladder and admired the book's leather cover.

Fascinated, Hawkeye said, "This looks really old."

Twisting a pigtail around her finger, Amy wandered over. "Yeah, I bet you it's at least as old as your grandmother."

"Are you kidding? Much older. Boy, I'd sure like to buy it. Mrs. von Buttermore already gave me two of her rare books. With this one, I could start a real collection."

A bookstore employee appeared silently from the other room. He wore wire-rimmed glasses and had a big bushy beard and pale skin.

Pronouncing each word with care, almost in a whisper, he said, "Hello. Please be careful with that book. It's very valuable. I just acquired it yesterday. The store's owner will be very pleased when he returns from vacation."

Hawkeye bit his lip and then said, "How much does it cost?"

A slight smile on his face, the man said, "I'm afraid this book is extremely expensive. My boss usually handles the rare books, but I bought it from a stranger just yesterday, and I had to pay a great deal of money for it myself. More so than usual."

Amy was puzzled. "Why?"

"I'll show you," he said proudly.

The man stroked his beard, then lifted the valuable book out of Hawkeye's hands. As if it were an infant, he laid the book on a nearby table.

"This book was a gift from Mark Twain to his grandson." Almost reverently, the bookseller opened the front cover. "It is extremely valuable because it was inscribed and signed by Mark Twain himself."

Amy gasped. "Cool, Hawkeye. Take a look at that!"

Written in old ink in large, flowery handwriting was an inscription. Hawkeye read it once, frowned, and reread it. Something about it bothered him. He had written a report on Mark Twain for school last year, and had read a lot about him.

Suddenly, Hawkeye realized what was wrong.

"I'm sorry," he said to the clerk, "but you're nuts if you paid a whole bunch of money for that book just because it's signed."

WHY DID HAWKEYE THINK IT WAS WRONG TO HAVE PAID SO MUCH FOR THE BOOK?

Find the solution on page 91

The Adventures of

TOM SAWYER

1st Edition

To Tom Twain,
As you know, you were the
inspiration for Tom Sawyer.
I hope you like reading about
the adventures of your namesake.
Happy Birthday!
Love,
Grandpa.
Twain

"This book was a gift from Mark Twain to his grandson,"
said the bookseller.

The Mystery of the
Rainy Night
Robbery

"Boy, a lot of people sure come to the movies on discount night," said Hawkeye. "Even when it's raining."

Hawkeye and Amy were at the very end of a long line, huddled beneath an old, torn umbrella.

"Everyone's getting soaked, including me," said Amy as water leaked through Hawkeye's umbrella and dripped down the back of her sweatshirt.

"Hawkeye, why didn't you borrow your father's new umbrella instead of his antique one?"

"He was using it." Hawkeye smiled. "At least I've got one."

Amy glanced up through the holes to the rainy sky. "Or part of one, anyway."

Suddenly someone grabbed the umbrella out of Hawkeye's hand.

"Excuse me, kids," said a tall woman with a loud voice, "but could I share your umbrella with you?"

Before Hawkeye or Amy could answer, the woman lifted Hawkeye's umbrella way up over her head. Down below, rain splattered in on both sleuths.

"Hey, ma'am," said Amy, "we're getting a little wet down here."

"Oh, sorry, dearie," responded the woman. "Just get a little closer to me and I'm sure you'll be fine."

Hawkeye leaned back behind the woman and made a face.

Amy laughed and whispered into Hawkeye's ear, "A real weirdo."

Hawkeye and Amy finally got their tickets for *Amazon Adventure* and found great seats right in the middle of the third row.

"This is a perfect place." Hawkeye wiped off his glasses and looked up at the screen towering above him. "When you sit here, it feels like the screen is going to fall right over on you."

Hawkeye and Amy were so excited during the movie that they hardly ate any popcorn. When the lights came back on, they found themselves on the edges of their seats.

"Excellent, man," Hawkeye said. "Just excellent."

Amy grabbed a big handful of popcorn. "Yeah, it was great. And the quicksand scene was the best. I thought for sure that guy was a goner."

Hawkeye picked up his dad's umbrella and the two of them headed out the side exit.

"Wow, can you believe it?" Hawkeye opened his umbrella. "It's still pouring."

Outside, the tall woman came up alongside them. "What do you think, kids?" she said, grabbing Hawkeye's umbrella again. "Aren't jungle movies exciting? Africa's so interesting."

Hawkeye looked at Amy and they both rolled their eyes.

Suddenly Sergeant Treadwell appeared up ahead on the street.

"Ms. Malloy!" he shouted to the woman. "I'm glad I caught up with you. Your neighbor said you'd be here. I'm afraid I have some bad news for you. Let's go over here under this awning and get out of the rain."

"What is it, Sergeant?" She handed Hawkeye his umbrella and put her hands in her raincoat pockets. "What's happened?"

"Hi, Sarge," said Hawkeye and Amy. "What's going on?"

"Hi, Hawkeye and Amy. Well..." He turned to the woman. "There's been a robbery. I'm afraid someone has broken into your home."

"Ohhh, no! But what about the burglar alarm?" She took off her rain hat so she could hear better. "Did... did they steal anything?"

"Well," said Sergeant Treadwell with a long face, "if you had anything of value in your family-room wall safe, it's gone. The burglar alarm went off, but the thief still got away."

"My mother's jewelry was in that safe!" she cried. "Oh, no!"

"Was it insured?" asked Hawkeye. "That would help."

"Oh, I don't know." Ms. Malloy wiped her eyes. "No, I don't suppose it was. What a mess this is. My stepsisters want the jewelry and they're suing me for it. This is going to confuse everything."

"Sounds like those stepsisters are good suspects, Sarge," said Amy.

"Could be. One of the neighbors said she saw a woman entering the house about an hour ago. Just for the record," Sergeant Treadwell asked, "it wasn't you, was it?"

Ms. Malloy was shocked. "Me? Why, of course not. Why would I rob my own home? And besides, I was here at the movie the whole time. Just ask these two kids."

"Yeah, she was here," said Amy, nodding.

Hawkeye snapped his fingers. "Uh-oh, Amy, I left my movie discount card in the theater." He took her by the arm. "Come on and help me find it before the next show starts."

"What? Oh, sure," said Amy. They hurried off.

When they got around the corner, Hawkeye stopped and took his pad and pencil out of his back pocket. "I didn't really lose my card, Amy. That was an excuse. I think Ms. Malloy knows more about the robbery than she's letting on. My sketch pad is a little wet, but I want to draw Ms. Malloy the way she looked when we first saw her."

"I want to draw Ms. Malloy the way she looked when we first saw her," Hawkeye said.

WHY DID HAWKEYE SUSPECT THAT MS. MALLOY KNEW SOMETHING MORE ABOUT THE ROBBERY?

Find the solution on page 93

The Mystery of
Amy's
Disappearance

Early one Friday night, the day before his birthday, Hawkeye sat on the edge of his bed trying to master a hand-held video game. With increasing success, Hawkeye was beating the machine at its own game.

He was so involved in the game that he failed to notice when the bright fall day turned into a dark evening. Hawkeye sat in the dark, with not even one lamp turned on.

Suddenly, something caught his eye. Once. Twice. Three times. There was a pause. Then the beam of light from Amy's house repeated itself. Once. Twice. Three times.

Hawkeye jumped up. That was the signal to come over—something big was up. Excited, Hawkeye hurried out.

"Mom, Dad!" he called as he raced out the door. "I'll be at Amy's!"

"Okay," they yelled back, but Hawkeye was already at the street. He had barely finished putting on his soccer jacket by the time he reached Amy's window. He grabbed a couple of pebbles from the ground next to her house and tossed them against the glass. Two pebbles later, Amy's kid sister came to the window and opened it.

"Lucy," said Hawkeye, looking up, "where's Amy?"

Lucy, a blonde six-year-old who was still missing her front teeth, shrugged. "Amy? I dunno. She just left."

"What do you mean she just left? She just signaled me to come over. I thought we had a new case to solve or something."

"Beat*th* me." Lucy had trouble with the letter 's.' "I *th*aw her in the family room before. Then she came running up here and told me there wa*th* big trouble. She just left. Maybe you better look for her."

Hawkeye didn't get it at all. Scratching his head, he asked, "Didn't she say anything else?"

"Oh, yeah. Um, she *th*aid... um, well... she *th*aid, 'Fir*th*t look acro*th*, and last look down.' "

"What? 'First look across, and last look down?'" Hawkeye shook his head. "Why did she signal me to come over and then leave? Lucy, can you let me in? Maybe there's a clue in the family room."

Lucy nodded. "Okay, Hawkeye. I'll be right there." With a bit of effort, she cranked the window shut.

A couple of minutes later, Hawkeye followed Lucy into the house. He took out his pad and pencil and looked all over the family room.

"This sure is weird," said Hawkeye. "I don't see anything."

Lucy frowned. "Well, she wa*th* in here. We better keep looking. I betcha we'll find *th*omething."

They searched under the couch, the coffee table, and even the rocking chair. Hawkeye looked for some sort of book or address or telephone number—anything that might tell him where Amy was. But he still couldn't find anything.

"Beats me where she is," he said, shrugging. "I'm kind of worried. I guess we'll just have to wait for a phone call. I sure hope she's not in danger."

Lucy fiddled with her ponytail, thought for a moment, and then said, "Hey, Hawkeye, what about the cro*th*word puzzle Amy was making up?"

Lucy picked up a pad of paper with a homemade crossword puzzle on it and showed it to Hawkeye. At first he was confused. Then a smile spread over his face as he realized where he could find Amy.

"Got it!" He jumped up and started outside. "Lucy, catch you later. Thanks for the help. I might get grounded for this, but a case is a case and a friend is a friend."

She hurried after him. "Hey, what about me?" she said, but Hawkeye didn't seem to hear her. When he was halfway out the door, she muttered, "Well, it sure took you long enough."

A split second later Hawkeye was gone. He hurried back to his house, grabbed his bike, and took off into the night.

WHERE DID HAWKEYE GO?

Find the solution on page 97

ACROSS

. _____ coaster
2. groovy priest
4. young dog
5. underground animal
7. repetition of your voice
9. _____ Pole
11. where money is kept
13. ___, ___, ___, your boat
14. old form of transportation
16. hamburger _____
17. bird's home
19. famous clown
21. Boy star of musical set in London
24. What a tailor does

DOWN

1. carpet
3. beneath
6. official standing
8. abode
10. Right _____
12. opposite of old
14. modest
15. what you sing
18. throw
20. car's nickname
22. liquid for a pen
23. smooth surface for skating

		²R	O	L	L	E	R			
²G	³U	R	U				⁴P	U	P	P	Y
	N	⁵G	O	P	H	E	⁶R			
	D						A			
	⁷E	C	⁸H	O			⁹N	O	R	¹⁰T	H
	R	O	11B	A	¹²N	K			T	
		U			E			¹³R	O	W
¹⁴H	O	R	S	¹⁵E	'S		W		¹⁶B	U	N
U		S	E		O					
M			¹⁷N	E	S	¹⁸T				
¹⁹B	O	Z	²⁰O		G		²¹O	L	²²I	V	E	²³R
L			L		²⁴S	E	W	S		N		I
E			D				S		K		N
			S							K

"Hey, Hawkeye," Lucy said, "what about the crothword puzzle Amy was making up?"

The Case of the
Sloppy
Vandals

With Amy's uncle at the wheel, they whizzed through the countryside.

"This convertible sure is cool," said Hawkeye from the back seat. He patted Nosey, whose ears were flapping madly in the wind. "You kind of like this, don't you, Nosey girl?"

"I love it," said Amy, the wind rushing through her hair. "Uncle Rick, it sure is great of you to take us fishing. I love being at your cabin."

"The pleasure's all mine," said her uncle, a thirtyish, bearded man. He was an editor for an outdoor-sports magazine, and he spent nearly every weekend outside.

Hawkeye said, "Too bad Sarge couldn't come. He's still busy with the paperwork from the video game theft. He's a great fisherman, even though he's kind of klutzy."

"That's for sure. He's always wrecking his equipment." Amy reached over and picked up a can of worms. "Oh, cool! Look at the size of these night-crawlers. They're huge!"

They rode in Uncle Rick's shiny red convertible for almost an hour. The car zoomed through rolling fields of corn and then came upon a hilly area dotted with lakes. Finally, they entered a forest so thick that the trees made a tunnel. A bit later, Uncle Rick turned off the main road and onto a narrow dirt lane. The trees began to thin.

"There's the cabin!" cried Amy, spotting the small house ahead. "And the lake. Look, it's so blue!"

Uncle Rick frowned. "What happened? It looks like someone's been here."

Hawkeye sat up as they approached the cabin. "I'll say."

As they drove closer, they could see that someone had broken into the little lakeside cabin. A window was shattered, the door was ajar, and garbage had been strewn all over the yard.

Uncle Rick stopped the car and stared ahead in shock. "Look at the mess. This is terrible."

Amy jumped out of the car. "What kind of creeps would do this?" she said angrily.

Hawkeye and Nosey climbed out of the car, too. "Wow. Whoever did this sure was a slob."

"You can say that again. I knew Sarge should've come."

Uncle Rick sadly shook his head and shrugged. "I guess I'd better call the police."

As Nosey ran off into the woods, Hawkeye pulled out his pad and pencil. "Meanwhile, we'll do what we can. Come on, Amy, let's check this out. These slobs left clues all over the place."

"Right. I see a couple already."

As Uncle Rick went in to call the police, Hawkeye sat down on a nearby stump and started to draw. Amy paced back and forth and called out the details one by one.

"Hey, Hawkeye," she said, pointing to the ground by the campfire. "Look at this scrap of burnt paper! And what about this... and this... and..."

The drawing was complete by the time Uncle Rick returned from calling the police.

"We found a bunch of stuff." Amy handed the sketch to her uncle.

"I'll say you did." His eyes opened in amazement. "This is sure to help the police."

"Amy and I found lots of clues," said Hawkeye. "We can figure out a lot about the people who were here, and I think we might even be able to find them."

WHAT CLUES DID HAWKEYE AND AMY DISCOVER, AND HOW DID THEY KNOW HOW TO FIND THE VANDALS?

Find the solution on page 101

"These slobs left clues all over the place," said Hawkeye.

The Secret of the
Ancient
Treasure

Part 3
The Mysterious Message

What Happened in Volumes 1 and 2
When Hawkeye and Amy were looking for fossils in
a cave along Mill Creek, they discovered an old metal
box buried deep in one of the underground rooms.
Inside the box was a yellowed, frayed map, which
clearly led to the von Buttermore estate. On the map
were some mysterious letters and numbers written in
code. Amy broke the code, which led them to Stall 3
in the old stable on the von Buttermore estate.

Mrs. von Buttermore guessed that the map was connected with the theft, eighty years ago, of her grandfather's priceless collection of ancient Egyptian gems and statuettes. Hawkeye, Amy, and Mrs. von Buttermore searched the stall for a clue that would lead them to the treasure.

At the end of "The Secret Room" (Part 2 of "The Secret of the Ancient Treasure"), Hawkeye noticed something out of place in a sketch he had done of the stable.

"Hey, I see something and I bet you it's the clue we're looking for!"
said Hawkeye.

The Mysterious Message

"Hey, guys, I think I found something, too," said Amy, tapping the floor.

But in his excitement, Hawkeye didn't hear her. "Mrs. von Buttermore, what's that candleholder doing there? Up by your hand."

"This?" She reached out and touched it. "I don't know. Why in the world would anyone put a candleholder in a place where there was so much straw? Heavens, it must have been a terrible fire hazard." She started to fiddle with it.

"Hey, you guys," shouted Amy, still knocking on the floor. "It sure sounds like there's nothing under this—"

Suddenly, as the candlestick twisted in Mrs. von Buttermore's hand, there was a sharp, screeching noise and Amy screamed.

"Help! He-elp!"

"What on earth?" said Mrs. von Buttermore, spinning around.

"She's disappeared!" gasped Hawkeye.

Right where Amy had been standing was a gaping hole. The floor had opened when Mrs. von Buttermore turned the candlestick.

Hawkeye pointed to it. "It's a trap door!"

Mrs. von Buttermore cried out and put her hand over her mouth. "Oh, my, my, my! Amy! Amy! Are you all right, dear?"

They rushed to the edge of the trap door and peered down. Sprawled out below on a pile of hay, the top of her red head swiveling around, was Amy.

Almost afraid to hear the answer, Hawkeye called, "Amy, are you all right?"

She tipped her head backward and looked up at them. Her voice a little shaky, she said, "Hey, wow..." A grin gradually emerged on her face. "What happened? The floor just fell right out from under me."

Hawkeye and Mrs. von Buttermore started to laugh with relief.

"Far out," sighed Hawkeye.

Mrs. von Buttermore said, "Don't you mean far down? She fell at least ten feet."

"I mean, cool." Hawkeye leaned carefully over the opening. "Amy, Mrs. von Buttermore just turned the candleholder and the trap door opened. It must have been some kind of secret lever."

"Well, thanks to all this hay, I had a soft landing," Amy replied.

"Hawkeye," said Mrs. von Buttermore, "toss her the flashlight so she can see better."

He dropped it to her. "Do you see anything? Do you see any Egyptian stuff?"

Amy flicked on the light and peered around the room from where she sat. "Ah, no. Nothing. Hey, there's a tunnel that leads off from here and... yes! Oh, my gosh! Hawkeye, Mrs. von Buttermore! Quick, hurry! There are some gold things down here!"

Hawkeye and Mrs. von Buttermore glanced at one another, gasped, and then dashed out of the stall. A moment later, they returned with a ladder.

"I can't believe it." Mrs. von Buttermore's eyes glowed with the thrill of it all. "After all these years, we might recover Grandpapa's Egyptian collection. Oh, isn't this exciting? Isn't this super? Tell me, Hawkeye, are all your cases this fun?"

"Well... kind of, but not really."

They swung the long wooden ladder around, stuck it through the trap door, and slid it down until it hit the floor of the secret room.

"You first, Mrs. von Buttermore," said Hawkeye. I'll hold the ladder."

Flushed with excitement, Mrs. von Buttermore gathered her flowing sari in one hand, lifted it, and began to climb down. Amy aimed the flashlight upward, and then helped Mrs. von Buttermore off the ladder. The two of them braced the ladder for Hawkeye, who practically slid down it.

Mrs. von Buttermore gazed around her in amazement. "A secret room. I always thought that's what this estate needed."

"Not only that," said Amy, pointing to a corner. "There's a secret passage, too."

Hawkeye stepped off the ladder. "Awesome!"

The room was small, perhaps only ten by twelve feet. Dust as dense as volcanic ash covered everything.

Mrs. von Buttermore put her fist to her chin. "Why, I bet you no one has been in this room since Dr. T stole Grandpapa's things. And that was almost eighty years ago."

"Amy, where's the stuff?" asked Hawkeye.

"Right there."

The beam of light landed on a shelf. Even through the thick dust, the gold sparkled and danced. None of them could speak for a moment. This was the stolen treasure—or at least part of it.

"To tell you the truth," said Hawkeye, his voice a little squeaky, "I don't think Amy and I have had such an exciting case in a long time."

Amy nodded slowly. "A real, real long time."

Mrs. von Buttermore stepped forward and, as if they were forbidden objects, hesitantly touched the gold necklace, the earrings, and the small gold statuette. They glowed with buttery warmth.

"Hey, look!"

Hawkeye pointed to a sign propped up behind the golden treasures. It was covered with pictures.

"Hey," said Amy, "that's a—oh, what's that word?—a rebus! You know, a picture code."

Squinting through her bifocals, Mrs. von Buttermore examined the sign. "My word, Amy, you're right. That's exactly what it is."

She pointed to the gold objects. "I'm certain these are only a few of the things that were stolen. I wonder if—"

"If the rebus will tell us where the rest of the Egyptian treasures are hidden!" exclaimed Hawkeye.

Mrs. von Buttermore's eyes lit up and she clenched her fists. "Maybe this rebus was another message from Dr. T to Jesse Carter. Perhaps Dr. Thomas really was in cahoots with Carter. If he couldn't get away with the treasure, maybe he thought a professional thief like Jesse Carter could."

"And maybe," said Amy, "Jesse Carter was arrested before he could get them."

Hawkeye glanced down the long, deep passage. "That might mean the rest of the treasure is down there somewhere."

Amy stepped forward and wiped the dust from the rebus. "Come on, we've got to figure this thing out."

Mrs. von Buttermore pulled on her earring. "Well, let me see. The first thing has something to do with tennis—was tennis around eighty years ago?"

"Oh, yes," said Hawkeye. "Hmmm. The second has to do with bugs."

"Look," said Mrs. von Buttermore. "There's an eye."

Hawkeye pointed. "And there's a word."

Meanwhile, Amy was working on her own. "Wait!" she gasped. She mouthed a sentence, pointing to the pictures in turn.

"That's it! I know what the rebus says! I know where we go!"

"Maybe the rebus will tell us where the Egyptian treasures are hidden!" exclaimed Hawkeye.

WHAT DOES THE REBUS SAY?

For the solution to this story and the conclusion to "The Secret of the Ancient Treasure" see *The Case of the Mysterious Dognapper*, Volume 4 in the **Can You Solve the Mystery?**™ series.

Solution

The Case of the
Computer
Camp Kidnap

"The kidnappers have Paul at the Haven Motel in Room One," said Hawkeye.

Hawkeye had noticed a pattern in the ransom note. Some of the letters were capitals and these formed the coded message.

Within minutes, the police arrived at the camp. They followed Hawkeye's directions, and safely rescued Paul and arrested the kidnappers at the nearby motel.

Paul said later, "The kidnappers made me write the ransom note while they kept watch. My dad specializes in secret computer codes, so when I was writing the note, I made up a code of my own."

The rest of camp was more fun than Hawkeye and Paul had imagined. The kidnappers, later prosecuted by Hawkeye's father, were found guilty and given a long prison sentence.

Solution

The Secret of the
Tomato Pincher

"Amy," said Hawkeye, waving his drawing, "that guy said he didn't like tomatoes. He said he was allergic to them. But if he's allergic to them, then why was he eating a hot dog with ketchup?"

"Ketchup?" asked Amy.

"Yeah, he had a big bottle of ketchup by his dinner plate. And ketchup is practically pure tomatoes!"

Amy snatched the drawing from Hawkeye's hands. "You're right, Hawkeye—we'll have cheese and tomato sandwiches for lunch tomorrow, after all!"

Solution

The Mystery of the
Unknown Rescuer

Only someone who worked at the library would have known the building well enough to have helped Mrs. von Buttermore. She had spoken with a number of people who worked there, but whoever helped her had to be someone nearby in the basement.

"The only person who could have helped you," said Hawkeye to Mrs. von Buttermore, "is a person who could find her way through the building with her eyes shut. And that's the woman at the information desk."

Amy gasped. "You're right, Hawkeye! She knows the library backwards and forwards and has it memorized because she's blind. It doesn't make any difference to her if the lights are on or off."

Hawkeye was indeed right, and Mrs. von Buttermore at once wrote a thank-you note to the woman.

The next day, Hawkeye, Amy, and the two women had a "little" eight-course banquet luncheon while Mrs. von Buttermore's dog Priceless and Star, the seeing-eye dog, played together outside on the lawn of the von Buttermore mansion.

Solution

The Case of the
Video Game Smugglers

With his good eye for detail, Hawkeye picked out the two thieves.

Hawkeye noticed that Suspect X in the photo had a hooked nose. When he looked at his sketch of Suspect #3, he realized that the man's nose wasn't hooked, even though he looked like Suspect X otherwise. But Suspect #1 did have a hooked nose. When Hawkeye looked closer, he realized that Suspect X had shaved his beard, cut his hair, and taken off his glasses.

Then Hawkeye looked closely at Suspect Y and saw that he had a very round face. Suspect #5 also had a round face. He also had shaved his head and put on glasses.

Hawkeye pointed to the sticker on the directory that Suspect #5 was carrying. "Amy! I bet that sticker covers a secret compartment—and that's where the video game flash drive is hidden."

Amy, bending over the sketch pad, saw it, too.

"You're right, Hawkeye! That's the case Suspect X was carrying before—only the sticker has been turned around. They didn't realize that it wasn't in the same position when they hid our flash drive under it."

Sergeant Treadwell arrested the two suspects and found the stolen video game drive hidden under the sticker. When the drive was returned to the computer club, the students sold the game and bought two new computers for the school.

Solution

The Mystery at
Mill Creek Bridge

Jamie was on his way to choir practice at school when he supposedly hit something and rode his bike off the bridge.

Hawkeye said, "But, Jamie, if that had really happened, how could you have landed down here near the river when your bike landed way up on the bank?"

Jamie hung his head and groaned, "Oh, bummer." He admitted that he had faked the accident to get out of choir practice.

"Come on, Jamie," said Hawkeye, "you might get out of choir practice today, but not tomorrow. Why don't you just be honest with your mom and tell her you'd rather do a different after-school activity?"

"Yeah, I suppose you're right. You know, I never told her I really want to learn to play the drums."

The very next week, Jamie started drum lessons, and the next month, his parents bought him a drum set for his birthday.

Solution

The Secret of the
Author's Autograph

Hawkeye knew the book was a fake. Mark Twain wrote many wonderful books, but he wrote them under a pen name. His real name was Samuel Clemens. Hawkeye said, "I don't know what Mark Twain's grandson's real name was—or even if he had a grandson—but I'm sure it wasn't Tom Twain. It had to be Clemens or something else. 'Grandpa Twain' sounds a little funny, too."

The clerk ripped off his glasses and covered his eyes with his hands. "Oh, no! I paid so much money for this book just yesterday. Of course it's a fake! How dumb of me! My boss is going to be furious!"

The clerk apologized profusely to Hawkeye and offered to sell him the book at a much lower price. Hawkeye suggested that, instead, he and Amy first do some sleuthing and track down the con man who sold the book to the Wise Owl Used Bookstore.

Solution

The Mystery of the
Rainy Night Robbery

Hawkeye suspected that Ms. Malloy knew something more about the robbery because she was dressed differently after the movie than she was before it. Before the movie, Ms. Malloy was wearing a dress, a short jacket, walking shoes, and a scarf. After the movie, however, she was wearing a hat, raincoat, and boots.

"The thing that got me thinking," said Hawkeye, "was that she thought movies about the African jungle were so exciting. But the movie was about the Amazon jungle, and the Amazon jungle is in South America, not Africa."

"Hey, you're right, Hawkeye," said Amy. "Ms. Malloy must have slipped out the exit door at the beginning of the movie. Then she went home, robbed her own safe, and joined us outside the movie theater after the film was over. The only mistake she made was changing her clothes because of the rain."

When Sergeant Treadwell asked her about this later, Ms. Malloy admitted that she had stolen the family jewelry.

"I wasn't going to accuse my stepsister and I wasn't going to try and get any insurance money, either," she pleaded. "I just didn't want to give up the jewelry."

Sergeant Treadwell warned Ms. Malloy about taking the law into her own hands, and she promised she would never make the same mistake again.

Solution

The Mystery of
Amy's Disappearance

Hawkeye went where Amy's instructions told him to go.

When he looked at the crossword puzzle, Hawkeye repeated Amy's instructions: "First look across, and last look down.".

Hawkeye saw that the first word across was "roller" and the last word down was "rink". From these clues, he guessed that Amy was at the Roll'nBowl Roller Rink.

He hopped on his bike and pedaled there as fast as he could. When he opened the door to the roller rink, it was black inside. But suddenly, all the lights came on, and Hawkeye's friends jumped up and down, waving their arms.

"Surprise!" they all shouted. "Happy birthday, a day early!"

A few minutes later, Lucy and Hawkeye's parents arrived with a box of presents and an enormous cake.

Lucy, quite proud of herself, said, "I wath pretty good, huh, Hawkeye? You didn't figure out that I wath thuppoth to get you here, did you? Amy was right—we could trick you!"

Solution

The Case of the
Sloppy Vandals

Hawkeye and Amy figured that the vandals must have come on two motorcycles because the tire tracks were not always parallel. And they must have come that morning, because they had left behind the Saturday edition of the newspaper. The vandals got into the cabin by breaking a window, reaching in, and unlocking the door.

Among other things, while they were there they had obviously built a fire and had a meal of hot dogs, potato chips, and watermelon. There were only three plates on the picnic table, so there probably only three vandals.

The burned receipt from Paul's Garage was the major clue. The police contacted Paul's Garage and learned that a man named Allen Lund had brought his motorcycle in for repairs on Friday. His fingerprints matched some of those found inside the cabin. Two days later, Lund, his girlfriend, and another man were arrested for the break-in.

The Girls to the Rescue Series

Edited by Bruce Lansky

Here are seven collections of stories featuring heroic, clever, and determined girls from around the world. Each book contains tales about girls such as Emily, who helps a runaway slave and her baby reach safety and freedom, and Kamala, a Punjabi girl who outsmarts a pack of thieves. This series for girls ages 7 to 13 has received critical acclaim and raves from mothers and daughters alike.

Can You Solve the Mystery Series

Twelve-year-old amateur sleuths and best friends Hawkeye Collins and Amy Adams love to solve cases. They invite readers to follow clues and sketches to solve crimes in their hometown of Lakewood Hills. All of the books in the Can You Solve the Mystery? series contain 9-10 short mysteries. Readers are given written and visual clues to help them solve the crime. The answers and a brief wrap-up are given in the back of the book. This series is for curious children ages 6 to 13.

◪ Meadowbrook Press

6110 Blue Circle Drive, Suite 237, Minnetonka, MN 55343

www.MeadowbrookPress.com